D1558313

Everything Is OK.

Love, God

Written by Heather Momper Leonard
Illustrated by Barbara Widmeyer Trauth

LifeRich Publishing is a registered trademark of The Reader's Digest Association, Inc.

LifeRich Publishing books may be ordered through booksellers or by contacting:

LifeRich Publishing
1663 Liberty Drive
Bloomington, IN 47403
www.liferichpublishing.com
1 (888) 238-8637

ISBN: 978-1-4897-2089-4 (sc)
ISBN: 978-1-4897-2088-7 (hc)
ISBN: 978-1-4897-2090-0 (e)

Printed in the United States of America.

LifeRich Publishing rev. date: 04/29/2019

For my children, anyone searching, and all those who have lost someone dear to them.

Dedicated to Nora Rose Yusko

When I was little, we
did everything with my
grandparents. They took
care of me when my parents
needed help, and they came
over for dinner every Sunday.
They played with me, sang
to me, and cheered me on.

4

When I was twelve years old, my grandpa was in the hospital for a long time. I asked my mom, "Why is grandpa so sick? Will he be ok?"

My mom explained, "Rebecca, I know this is difficult, but grandpa is very old and nearing the end of his life. We need to think of all of our good times with him and begin to say goodbye."

I did not want to believe
my mom. I thought my
grandpa would live forever.
I said a prayer that night:
"God, please do not take
my grandpa to heaven."

8

The next day at school, my teacher talked to me about losing his dad. He told me how sad it made him but that he also felt comforted by something. He said that there are signs from our loved ones in heaven being sent to us on Earth all of the time. He said that whenever he sees a dime all by itself, he knows it is from his dad. Whenever he sees certain numbers in a row, he feels it is a sign from God that He is there for him. He called these signs **"God moments."**

My teacher made me think of all the times my parents told me to look for God reaching out to me. They always said that He could come to me in many forms and that loved ones who are with Him would do the same. My mom said whenever she sees a rainbow, it is her mom reaching out to her. My dad said that hummingbirds visit him, and they are a sign from his brother in heaven. My parents told me that the signs always come, even if they take a while.

The next day, I visited
my grandpa and told him
how much I loved him.

Later that night, my grandpa died. How could this be? I was not ready for him to die. What about my prayer? I asked my dad, "Why would God do this when I prayed and prayed for Him not to?"

My dad explained that God surely saved grandpa from further suffering and gave him peace that would last forever. He told me, "Rebecca, God is good all the time, even if we are hurt by what is happening in our lives. Grandpa is happier than he has ever been with God. Always remember that grandpa still loves us from heaven."

In bed that night, I cried and cried. I thought of the many walks I took with my grandpa. He would tell me to make a wish whenever we saw a ladybug. Through all of my tears, I prayed that God would send me a sign that grandpa was with Him and everything was ok. I prayed and prayed that God and grandpa would send me ladybugs.

I waited.

Two days later, as family and friends gathered at the house, I went to my room. I was so sad and wanted to be alone. I just could not imagine my life without my grandpa in it. He had loved me so much. He had always been there for me. As I cried into my pillow, I felt something crawling on my hand. I sat up and saw a big red ladybug on my hand!

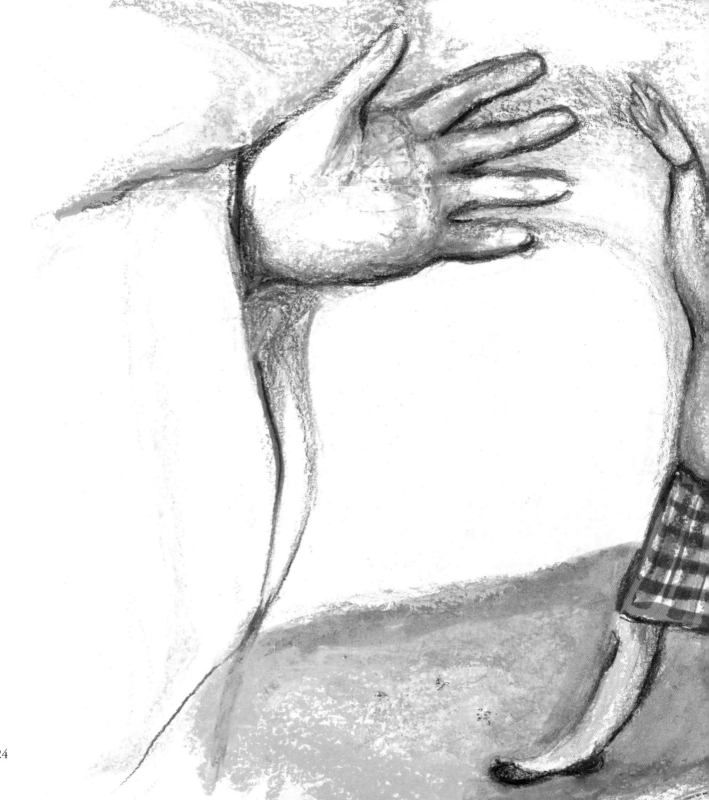

24

There it was! I was not dreaming. I thought, *I am not alone. Grandpa is with me, and God is with me, even when I cannot see either of them!* This was what I had prayed for. This ladybug seemed to tell me,

"Everything is OK....Love, God."

The next day, at the funeral, I was walking into church with my parents, and my dad said, "Rebecca, there is a ladybug on your shirtsleeve." He started to brush it off.

I stopped him and told my parents all about my prayer and what had happened the night before. They wiped away their tears, and we all hugged.

A few months later, in the lunchroom at school, a ladybug was crawling on my lunchbox. "Wow!" I yelled, surprised.

My friends asked me why I was smiling so much. I told them about the ladybugs.

Three of my friends immediately told me their own stories of God moments.

Nora told me how she says a prayer every time she sees a heart because she knows it is God reaching out to her. She sees heart shapes everywhere—in the clouds, the leaves fallen from a tree, a rock, her food, and even a bruise on her leg.

Sean said he hears a certain song and knows it is a sign from his grandpa.

Mae said she sees cardinals and feels they are her mom visiting her from heaven to let her know she is always there, watching over her.

I was so glad that I told my friends about the ladybugs. It felt so good to hear their stories. I remembered that before my grandpa's funeral, my mom told me, "We have to be brave and have faith that this is not the end, Rebecca."

Now I look around me, and I feel there is so much more than I used to see. I still miss my grandpa every day. But I know that grandpa is watching over me and God is telling me,

"Everything is OK."

I wrote this book for my children and they have pushed me to share it with you.

The story comes from a special place in my heart. Several years ago, our daughters were begging us for a brother. It made me think of the baby boy we lost when we first got married. Miscarriages are so common and I knew people who had lost older children, so I never felt the right to mourn. But I was still so sad to have never met our baby.

One day, I prayed to God and our baby in heaven for a sign that they are together. I prayed for ladybugs. The first ladybug came to me within days. Soon, each of my daughters came to me with ladybugs from the most unlikely places. I finally told them about their brother in heaven and my prayer. For several years now, my children tell me every time they see a ladybug. They have grown up with these beautiful God winks and they feel such comfort. Whenever the ladybugs find me, I am reassured and filled with hope. I have spoken with many friends who have their own signs from God and loved ones in heaven. Their stories inspire me and are a very special part of the story "Everything is OK. Love God."

I hope this book can encourage others to look for signs from heaven so that when they face struggles, they know they are never alone. God is real and our loved ones are safe and sound with Him. Life can be so hard, but God is always trying to make it easier for us. He wants us to pray, pay attention and share our stories of God moments in our lives.

What is your story?

www.everythingisokloveGod.com

www.facebook.com/pg/EverythingisOKLoveGod

instagram "everything_is_ok_love_god"

35

ABOUT THE AUTHOR

Heather Momper Leonard lives in Cincinnati, Ohio with her husband Brian and their four daughters, Grace, Caitlin, Nora and Maeve. Heather studied English and Psychology in College and has always enjoyed writing.

ABOUT THE ILLUSTRATOR

Barbara Widmeyer Trauth is an accomplished Artist. She is a Sculptor, Painter and Illustrator. Barbara lives in Cincinnati, Ohio with her husband, children and grandchildren.